Join us for *The Monster Guys Podcast!*

These stories were originally shared through our *Yokai Tales Podcast* episodes (part of *The Monster Guys Podcast*), followed by a brief discussion about each yokai. We continue to share original and classic stories from the rich tradition of Japanese folklore each month.

We also share in an ongoing conversation about monsters, folklore, and mythology in general. As well, we journey to far-off lands through our *Folk Tales Podcast* episodes (formerly known as *Faerie Tales Podcast* also part of *The Monster Guys Podcast*), and explore the folklore and mythology of the Fae-folk through story each month.

Subscribe to *The Monster Guys Podcast* through Apple Podcasts, Stitcher, YouTube, iHeartRadio, Google Play Music, Spotify, and many other places where you can download your favorite podcasts.

You can also find us at *TheMonsterGuys.com* or:

On FACEBOOK.COM/THEMONSTERGUYS

On TWITTER.COM/THEMONSTERGUYS

-D.C. & C. Michael McGannon, a.k.a., The Monster Guys

Yokai Tales

Stories from Japan's
Grand & Mysterious
Tradition of Folklore

YOKAI TALES

STORIES FROM JAPAN'S GRAND & MYSTERIOUS TRADITION OF FOLKLORE

狸

D.C. MCGANNON &
C. MICHAEL MCGANNON

ILLUSTRATED BY
D.C. MCGANNON

Redcap Studios

Yokai Tales:
Stories from Japan's Grand & Mysterious Tradition of Folklore

Written by D. C. McGannon & C. Michael McGannon

Illustrated by D. C. McGannon

Cover Layout by Matthew D. Smith (www.mdsmithdesign.com)

Copyright © 2018 by D.C. McGannon, C. Michael McGannon

Published by Redcap Studios, 2018
An imprint of The McGannon Group, Ltd. Co.

Yokai Tales: Stories from Japan's Grand & Mysterious Tradition of Folklore /
by D. C. McGannon & C. Michael McGannon — 2nd Ed.

Summary: A collection of stories bringing to life Japanese yokai in the tradition of fairy tales and ghost stories.

2   4   6   8   10   12   14   16   18

ISBN-13: 978-0-9861458-7-2

To Randy Stuhlsatz and Holly Crain, and our extended family at Anime Festival Wichita — every step has been a joy with you all!

Foreword

Over the past decade or so, there has been a huge surge in global awareness of Japanese folklore. These days Japan's ghosts and monsters can be found all over the internet, books, comics, television, and movies. Everyone—from individual independent writers to big-name studios—seems to be getting in on this explosion of folklore, contributing to the growing awareness. Words like yokai, mononoke, tengu, and kitsune are becoming common terms. It wasn't long ago that almost nobody knew about these things; today there are fans all over the world.

One of the key aspects of folklore is that it doesn't belong to anybody; it belongs to everybody. Each storyteller builds upon those who came before them, picking the parts they like best and adding their own bits and pieces to the story. This collection of short stories continues that tradition, starting with the traditional roots of Japanese folklore and retelling them for a modern audience. DC and Michael McGannon draw upon the "folk" nature of folklore by taking familiar stories and making them their own.

Their tales stay true to the nature of the ghosts and monsters of old Japan, while adding a bit of their own personality into the mix. Diehard fans of Japanese folklore will recognize the original folktales at the heart of each of these short stories.

DC and Michael McGannon's stories draw from and contribute to the ongoing resurgence of Japanese folklore. They are part of the shared tradition of storytelling which stretch from time immemorial and continues to this day.

-Matthew Meyer

www.Yokai.com

June 30, 2016

About The Art

Three words came to mind while I was sketching these yokai: *playful, experimental,* and a little bit of *chaos.*

I've never published any art before, so I am taking a big risk in doing so here. This is a new style for me altogether. I'm a doodler, a master of stick figures — at best. I am inspired by many modern yokai artists, but I wouldn't be able to stand in the same room with them. People like Matthew Meyer (from Yokai.com - go see for yourself) and Mark T. Morse (from TheGatelessGate.com / *Narrow Road* with Zack Davisson) are legends in my eyes! My goal here, like our story-telling, was to have some fun and enjoy learning about these yokai even more through art.

I enjoy the whimsy and the danger that encompass these monsters and their stories, and so I attempted, on a very simple level, to capture some of that. When I observe some of the art that accompanies Japan's classic folklore, I'm taken by its simplicity, and just how raw it is. I wanted to honor that tradition, and begin to explore these yokai even further myself through this medium.

The sketches are only a beginning, unfinished in a way, raw, playful.

I ask you to join me in enjoying them as such. As I continue to journey deeper into Japanese folklore in the future, my art will undoubtedly follow that path.

For now, you will have to put up with someone who is like a kid sitting at a table, drawing out their favorite monsters with a pencil, and dreaming up wild stories to go along with them. I hope you enjoy them (and maybe draw some monsters yourself)!

-D.C. McGannon

June 2016

釣瓶落とし

Illustration 1: Tsurube Otoshi

The Forest of 1000 Lights

by D.C. McGannon

Yokai: Tsurube Otoshi

One of the things I enjoy when reading Japanese fables is the subtlety (sometimes) of how creatures or spirits are introduced. And no matter how devastating, bloody, or disgusting their actions can be, the focus is not always on the "special effects" or the consequences that accompany their character and appearance, rather allowing the reader's imagination to fill in the blanks.

There are plenty of stories and writings about the Tsurube Otoshi that give vivid details with regards to the consequences levied on its victims, however I wanted to paint a contrasting picture of love and celebration, with a sudden "monstrous" entry that allowed room for the individual's imagination. I didn't want to linger on the violence, for I believe we can do that quite well on our own most of the time.

However, in true Japanese folklore tradition, often the stories end abruptly, painfully violent, sad, and without resolution. My western mind is slowly learning that that is okay in this tradition, and that these stories don't always have to make a point. Sometimes entertainment is its own value.

The Forest of 1000 Lights

by D.C. McGannon

The sun danced lightly across the treetops of the Forest of One Thousand Lights. The cheerful afternoon soon gave way to twilight, and even that unto the embrace of the darkness of the night. To the west, a well-traveled mountain pass slithered into the forest's belly like a snake in tall grass. The path led from a bustling village, and at one time was said to provide safe passage for people to bring their water buckets to be filled in one of the forest's many natural wells. But that was a time long since passed.

Today, mostly, the trail is used for leisurely strolls in the afternoon sun, or for early morning walking meditation. From time to time, lovers are known to skip along seeking the cover of the sprawling Kaya trees, boasting in the passions of one another's kisses.

The forest is so-named the *Forest of One Thousand Lights* because of the hypnotic splendor that it provides during the cycles of the full moon's light. For several days leading up to each month's full moon, and for several days following, the Celestial Queen's pale light strikes the waters in the forest's wells just so that it sends shimmers of lights glistening through the trees. It is a magical display, to be sure, and such an enchantment that the people of the village gather several times throughout the year for dancing and celebration at the forest's edge in honor of the lights.

During the fullest of moons, it's like watching cascades of fireworks bursting in the trees. And it is on these nights when legends were born and stories told.

Today, people believe them to be just that: *stories*. Nothing more than fables meant to frighten misbehaving children, or entertain those gathered around a crackling campfire.

Stories, however, have a way of weaving their way into our lives, preserving our histories, and revealing a life that still may exist but a stone's throw beyond the glistening lights of a modern landscape.

So it was, long ago, for two lovers who set out for a fateful midnight stroll.

Nearing the forest, the couple heard laughter. Maniacal cackling almost. Faint, distant. They dismissed it as a band of wayward teenagers out for a good stomp in the night.

As the laughter faded, lights began to illuminate the trees of the forest. Rhythmically skipping from tree to tree as though they were enticing passers-by to join in the dance.

And join in the dance, the two lovers did.

The intensity of their swaying and whirling was met only by their unabashed mirth.

Until . . .

They found themselves at the forest's edge. Silent. Breathless. *Still.*

The lights, too, had come to a halt. Each seemed to be waiting on the other's cue to continue their performance.

Then it happened . . .

The flicker of a single light bounced through the trees.

Then a second, and a third . . .

Until one thousand lights were flittering and prancing from branch to branch in a dazzle of delight and whimsy. It was an intoxicating invitation to join the lights in their dance under the pale moon light.

And that is precisely what the star-crossed lovers did.

Upon entering the forest, the two young romantics no longer tittered about, but found themselves in total darkness.

The lights had shuttered suddenly, and the laughter returned. The voices echoed in their calamitous shrieks and monstrous taunts. The lovers became confused and separated, yelling in terror — lost and crying out for one another's embrace.

Reaching the climax of their incessant squawks and gabbles, the voices gave way to paralyzing silence. The lights of the forest returned in a dizzying spectrum as the petrified couple found each other's gaze, realizing they had never been further than an arm's length away from each other.

With the rush of a violent wind, a voice that could only be described as an earthquake falling from the sky boomed with the command, "HEADS UP!"

In an instant, the two lovers looked to the treetops to see a giant face, the size of a mountain boulder, crashing through the branches, only a moment before the disembodied demon's head crushed them under its weight. What hadn't been crushed by the gigantic head was quickly consumed by a pack of smaller bird-like heads.

For a waning moment, the laughter and cackling continued until only the tearing of flesh and the crunching of bones could be heard. A moment later, the forest fell silent, at peace.

In a nearby bar, a late night crowd felt the earth tremor and paused in their drinking, thinking back to the stories of old. But it was a passing thought. One old man cheered and raised his glass, and the rest of the bar followed happily, for earthquakes and thunderstorms were common in their region, and it was a time long since passed when monsters were to blame for common science. Now, both fable and science alike were simply excuses to drink until the wells of overindulgence ran dry.

野箆坊

Illustration 2: Noppera Bo

Faceless

by C. Michael McGannon

Yokai: Noppera Bo

The Noppera Bo seems harmless enough on the surface. But being a monster that can wipe away, and practically shapeshift her face, she is all about the scares. Particularly the ones that leave you a babbling mess in your own home.

Throughout this collection, there are a handful of stories that were directly inspired by classic tales in Japanese literature. This is one of those stories, sticking close to an old formula built for the creepy factor.

In all honesty, Japanese ghost stories, or kwaidan, have always been able to bring on the chills. However, it does have a few twists that make it original and lend to a feeling of terror as our young hero discovers a monster that relishes the ultimate psyche-out . . .

Enjoy!

Faceless

by C. Michael McGannon

Children love their freedom. Often, this comes at the expense of the patience of their parents.

Kosuke was not a bad child by any stretch of the imagination. He was studious, kept himself active, and listened to his mother.

Usually.

But on occasion he did try her patience.

Kosuke loved to find different places to fish, as all adventurous boys should. He would explore the edges of his small world when there were no other duties to tend to at home.

On one such hot, boring day, Kosuke grabbed his fishing rod and a basket, humming to himself happily.

"Where are you going?" his mother asked, smiling at her son.

"I am going to fish!"

She laughed. "I can see that. Where do you intend to throw your line this time?"

Kosuke had found several spots to fish, but there was a particular place that had always held his intention, and one which he'd never felt brave enough to venture into. Old folks whispered about it, saying it was a place haunted by spirits and strange animals.

"There is a pond beyond the old hag's house," he told her, as vague as he could manage, for he was sure she would not approve of him going if she knew of which pond he spoke.

"Do not call her that, Kosuke! That's rude. *Wait.* The pond with the cherry blossom?"

He nodded slowly, eyes shifting to keep from meeting hers.

"Kosuke, you must not go there to fish, or visit that place for any reason. It is a haunted place. Please, find another place to fish today."

Kosuke hung his head and shuffled toward the door. "Yes, mother."

She watched him wander off before returning to her own tasks, still worried.

Outside, Kosuke took off running. The sun was

hot on his shoulders, but he didn't mind for the breeze. He passed several people he knew along the way, each one stopping to offer him a friendly greeting. He also passed his friend Nagisawa, a soba vendor, who sat snoring under the shade of his little vending stand.

"Nagisawa-san!" he yelled as he passed by, laughing as the elder sleeping man nearly fell from his seat in surprise.

"Kosuke, you rascal!" The white-haired man jokingly pounded the air with his fist.

When Kosuke had to pass the hag's house, he slowed. The woman who lived there was haggard and solitary, and always gave him the creeps. Some whispered that she was a witch who used a dog as her familiar, but no one dared try to prove the matter. He kept an eye on the darkness where her rice-paper door had been left open, waiting for the dog spirit to appear and fly at him. But it was silly superstition, and no evil spirits came after the boy. He laughed and called himself silly, then continued to run, perhaps a little faster than before.

The pond was not far beyond that, and he reached it quickly. It was a serene place, and it seemed the sun did not beat down quite as hot near the water here. The single cherry blossom tree provided shade and a calming rustle, in rhythm with the ripples upon the pond created by the wind and playful fish. Kosuke smiled at the peaceful atmosphere and set down his basket, readying his fishing rod. He reclined against the sheltering tree, and tossed his line.

So at peace was he, while waiting for the fish to take interest, that Kosuke allowed his eyes to close, a smile upon his small, round face. The warmth of the sun caused his mind to wander. The breeze sung him a lullaby, soothing Kosuke into a gentle nap.

When he woke, it was night and it was no longer warm. In fact Kosuke shivered, finding himself quite cold. His basket was gone, but he still held onto his fishing rod, which he now clung to.

"What are you doing here, child?"

Kosuke jumped, not having noticed the woman standing slightly to his right. She was dressed in white and blue and offered a kindly smile. "I came here to fish," he answered, fearful.

"Child, did you not know that it is unsafe to fish

here? It is said this place is sacred, kept by spirits."

"I've heard the rumor, miss. But, surely it's just a story."

The woman stepped closer, leaning down, eye-to-eye with the boy. "It is not just a story," she said with a smile. The woman reached up, fingers digging into her forehead, and with a smooth motion she wiped her face away. Before Kosuke stood a woman with an empty face, her skin as smooth as an egg.

Kosuke screamed and ran from the pond, dropping his fishing rod in a mad dash to escape this terror. He saw the old hag's house and pounded the earth with his feet as hard as he could, catching sight of a large dog watching from that empty blackness in the night. It only added to his haste.

"Kosuke! Kosuke, what's wrong!" cried Nagisawa from his soba stand.

"Nagisawa-san!" Kosuke leaned on his friend's booth. It didn't occur to him that Nagisawa did not keep his stand open this late at night. "You'll never believe it. I went fishing at the old pond with the big cherry blossom."

Nagisawa sat back in shock. "The haunted one?"

"Yes! I fell asleep in the warmth of the sun, and when I woke up there was a strange lady there. She told me it wasn't safe to fish there and then . . . and then . . . her face disappeared!"

Nagisawa's eyes were wide with surprise. "You mean, like *this*?" he asked, reaching up to wipe his face. When his hand dropped, Nagisawa's face was gone.

Kosuke fell back from the vendor's booth, scrambling away as Nagisawa's muffled laughter echoed in the night. The man's eerie cackle bounced off trees and through Kosuke's mind long after the soba stand was out of sight.

Finally, he made it home. Kosuke was unsure of what time of night it was, but his house was unusually dark. There was a faint glow coming from within, hardening the fear that sat in his stomach. He followed the glow into the house, around corners of rooms that should have been more familiar, and through the hallway. The light was coming from the kitchen. There, Kosuke's mother prepared the evening meal by the light of a single, flickering candle.

When he saw his mother, his fear melted away.

He ran to her, wrapping his arms around her tight.

"Kosuke! What's wrong, you look as if you've been crying."

"Mother, I went to the pond. I'm so sorry. You were right! It's a dangerous place, and I promise I'll never go there again."

She rubbed his back, looking him in the eye, concerned. "Tell me what happened, Kosuke."

"It was terrible . . ." he began.

Kosuke retold his story from beginning to end. About the warmth and peace of the small pond, about waking up at night, the stranger in blue and white, and then about how his friend Nagisawa had also wiped his face away right before his eyes.

His mother stopped him there. "That's horrible! So they took their faces off?" she asked. "Like *this*?"

To Kosuke's horror, his mother reached up and smoothed her hand over her face. She stared at him with eyeless, mouthless features, tilting her head just so, and Kosuke gasped. The single candle suddenly went out, throwing them into darkness.

さがり

Illustration 3: Sagari

An Old Fool's Warning

by C. Michael McGannon

Yokai: Sagari & Uma no ashi

Some yokai do not seem to take center stage very often. The sagari is one of those creatures. Many people know of it, but typically it is only mentioned or seen in passing. Yokai like the sagari are of a bizarre yet simply variety, and that is perfectly fine. In scary stories, there is much to be said for keeping things simple.

This story seeks to keep the sagari's simplicity, while giving it a spotlight to spread its grotesque charm among a wider audience.

The Uma no ashi also finds a cameo here. The thought of encountering either one of these face to face is certainly worthy of a few tingles in the spine.

An Old Fool's Warning

by C. Michael McGannon

A merchant had promised to deliver goods to the south. He passed through many towns, stopping one night in a small fishing village for rest. Checking into an inn, he secured his cart loaded with goods and led his faithful horse to the stables. Before bedding for the evening, he sat for a meager meal and a welcome drink. An old man with an unruly mop of hair, and a wild look in his eye, caught his attention. The man stared at the merchant at length before the wild-eyed man pat down his white kimono and abruptly exited the room. Soon after, the merchant forgot the matter entirely.

Later that night, the merchant heard screams and wails, setting his nerves on edge. Quickly, he rose and dressed himself, then walked outside the inn to see what the ruckus was about. It was the unruly man. His white clothing had become ruffled, and he waved a sword haphazard, yelling at the direction of the forest. A lean, confident man approached and disarmed the man, who continued to scream at the trees. Two more of the local townspeople helped to escort the crazy man away.

The merchant, bewildered, took hold of the innkeeper's shoulder, who had also come out to watch the commotion. He asked what pain or evil had fallen upon the old man.

"Oh, nothing," answered the innkeeper. "He's a drunken fool. He fought in the old war. They say a battle was fought in that very forest, and many men died there. But I wouldn't know. It was before my time."

Troubled, the merchant went back to bed, haunted by dreams of the old man screaming at him and his horse.

The next morning the merchant readied himself for the road.

"Where are you headed?" the innkeeper asked during a friendly conversation.

The merchant explained his route, mentioning

that he would pass through the dense forest to save time between towns.

The innkeeper grew quiet. Serious. "Do not go there," he said. "I beg of you, go around the forest. It is not safe."

The merchant laughed and waved off the innkeeper's fear. He had traveled much of Kyushu and could handle himself just fine.

He gave his horse a scratch behind the ears and sat in his cart, the road soon jostling him about in his seat. The next village was still a good distance away, so he determined to waste as little time as possible.

The forest was difficult to travel through, but not particularly dangerous as far as the merchant could see. Given the innkeeper's fear, he expected bandits or some other criminal faction to be hiding in the trees. There were none, only the turn of the wheel and the dull conversational skills of his horse.

Soon, the sun was prepared to dip beneath the horizon. The merchant grew weary and struck a fire, allowing himself a small meal. Satisfied, he went to sleep, trusting his horse to provide an alarm against danger. Again this night, the merchant was plagued with horrible dreams. This time he dreamt he was wandering among the trees, hearing the anguished whinnies of hundreds of horses.

The merchant woke with a terrible fever, shivering in the embrace of the warm night's soft breeze. Fully awake now, he could still hear a horse whinnying with terror. Fear struck the merchant, for he thought his horse was under attack by some forest-dwelling rogue. The merchant jumped to his feet and turned to face his companion.

Instead of being met with the sight of his own horse, he was met with the vision of a sickly horse's face. The disgusting beast screamed in his face, fetid breath turning his stomach. The merchant scrambled backward several steps and was horrified to see the horse head had no body. Instead, its shriveled neck hung limp and twisted midair, the whole of the beast's head hung by its ratty mane, tangled in the branches of the tree he had slept beneath.

The merchant cried out, terrified. He received a harsh blow between his shoulders, falling to the ground. Looking in the direction of his attacker, he saw a horse's leg hanging from the branches there, kicking and bucking at the air. His panicked gaze found more and more hanging from trees all around him. The forest was animated with dismembered horse legs and innumerable horse heads, all of which watched him, eyes so wide he could see the strained whites of each eyeball. The merchant was frozen in his fear, feeling more feverish with each passing moment.

Suddenly, the screams of a wild man became clear among the hellish cacophony of horse whinnies. The crazy old drunk came into view, screaming at the trees and waving his sword. The hanging horse heads swayed in response, agitated. The old man grabbed the merchant by his robes and shoved him toward his horse and cart.

"Go! Leave now!" cried the old drunkard.

Without the need for a second urging, the merchant hurled himself into the cart. His horse galloped violently, already having crossed the threshold of its own fear. The merchant braved a final look over his shoulder as he passed through the dark woods. The crazed man was still there, but he looked much younger now, sitting atop a horse in regal armor. A company of horses stood behind him, dressed for battle, each screaming their hellish whinnies, long dead.

When he arrived back in town, the merchant spoke nothing of what he saw with the villagers or the innkeeper. He arrived at the next town several days late, unwilling to pass through any forest ever again.

Illustration 4: Nukekubi

I've Lost My Head

by C. Michael McGannon

Yokai: Nukekubi

Here's another story inspired by an old legend. In fact, this story has been adapted and used by a few other writers, most notably in our modern era by Mike Mignola in his *Hellboy* series.

Much like in the *Hellboy* story, and much like the original priest in that far off old tale, the hero of this story is not your everyman. He's wily, serving to remind us that yokai are deadly, dangerous, and not to be trifled with, but also imperfect beings themselves who can, from time to time, be surprised and taken advantage of.

I've Lost My Head

by C. Michael McGannon

Isogai was a madman. Or at least the few that knew him thought him to be. He had been many things in life, and had gained much wealth, and traveled alongside many companions. But those were other lifetimes, and the Isogai of this time had left his weighty past behind.

A backpack slung over his shoulder, Isogai hiked through the Kai Mountains whistling an old wartime song, taking in the beauty around him.

It should be said, Isogai was well aware of the reputation of the Kai Mountains. Demons, goblins, and ghosts alike dwelled in the area, preying on those unfortunate enough to live nearby.

In his wandering, Isogai came to a strange house. It was strange in the fact that it seemed so normal in this dangerous and troubled region. Its warm, inviting presence amused Isogai and he passed it readily, more willing to spend his night under the treetops and with the monsters those trees undoubtedly hosted. He continued whistling his wartime tune, gray hair blowing carefree in the breeze. But the sun had already started to set, and Isogai was on the lookout for a place to rest his head. So when he heard the sound of an axe against wood, he went to look for company, not long after finding a man hard at work gathering logs.

The man jumped in fright, clinging to his axe, dull though it looked. "Goodness me! Who are you?"

"A simple wanderer," said Isogai. "Who are you?"

"A simple woodcutter."

The two men watched each other for a moment, wary of the other, before Isogai let out a hearty laugh. "I am sorry! I forget, these woods are said to be dangerous after all. I'll leave you to your woodcutting."

"No, wait! Forgive me. I can see that you are a simple traveler, and not a demon. Forgive me, but no goblin or demon would disguise himself as casually as you are dressed. But why would you come this way? Surely you are on a journey of some importance."

"Not at all. I wander. That is all. My name is Isogai."

"Takahashi. A pleasure to meet you! As a resident of this area, I can't simply turn a person away I suppose. There's no telling what would happen to you when night falls. My house is a humble thing, and I'm afraid we do not have much food to share, but it is a safer place than any within miles I can assure you."

"Thank you," said Isogai with a smile. "That is very kind of you. Here, let me help."

Together, the men set off, Isogai following Takahashi and helping to carry the bundles of wood. Isogai was hardly surprised when they came to Takahashi's house. It was the same cabin that he had passed earlier, seeming even brighter and friendlier than before.

"This is it," said Takahashi, taking the lead inside.

Several people were inside, reclining by a fire. They rose with excitement and some surprise at the sight of a guest. It was not often that people came this way, Isogai surmised.

"You are welcome here," said Takahashi. "I would prepare a great dinner for you, but our funds are low right now and the last few days we have had only water and some sake to get by with."

Isogai sympathized with the man. "How unfortunate. It seems strange . . . Your home is very nice, yet you find yourself in hard times."

"It's true. My friends and I used to be quite important people to a landowner not far from here. I fought to protect the region and was well known for it."

"Ah! A fellow soldier."

Takahashi smiled. "Yes! Always nice to meet a kindred soul. Sadly, I let the fame get the better of me. Sake and women, Isogai. They are a horrible combination when you lack self-control such as I did."

"I am sad to hear this. I will say a prayer for you and your friends here."

The group looked at Isogai with some confusion. "You would pray for us?" asked Takahashi.

"For a long time, I lived among Buddhist priests and learned some of their ways, some of their prayers. Perhaps I can bring this house some good fortune. After all, you took me in, so while indulgent I cannot see you being a horrible soul."

Takahashi seemed ashamed. "You are too kind, but I thank you. Please, make yourself at home tonight."

True to his word, Isogai stayed awake for some time that night after the others had gone to sleep. In his guest room, he had taken from his backpack a paper lantern and prayer beads. He watched the shadows carefully that night while reciting mantras for the good health of his hosts, ears pricked for any unusual sound. For, thankful as he was, Isogai suspected that not all was as it seemed.

It was late. Isogai had not yet slept, and now he rose from his prayers, deciding to go out into the house of the woodcutter. From his backpack he pulled a hanbo — a wooden staff a little over a foot in length — and slid open his door, stepping carefully into the shadows of the hallway.

As he had suspected, Isogai soon found himself in a house of horrors. There, by the now-dead fireplace he had seen lit so warmly earlier that night, laid the bodies of Takahashi and his housemates. Each was spread out like a ragdoll, missing their heads. But

Isogai was wise and did not panic, quickly noticing a distinct lack of blood anywhere in the room. He examined one of the bodies and noted how the headless neck was smooth, and clean.

Isogai spun the hanbo idly in his hand, his ears picking up the sound of chatter from outside where one of the sliding doors had been left open. He slung the body of Takahashi over his shoulder and walked outside, careful, quiet as a cat. There was a nasty chattering of voices from the trees behind the house. Isogai set the body down behind some bushes, making sure it was well hidden, before creeping closer to the source of the conversation.

"I wonder if he's done yet," a female voice whined. "I'm so hungry."

An angry male grunted. "Hmph! We've survived on insects and earth dwellers this long without a problem. I don't see why you had to bring a priest here! Food or no food, I hate having to wait outside."

"How was I to know he could recite the sutras?" cried Takahashi's voice, and Isogai saw him. There, flitting about the air, almost as if pacing, was Takashi's head, teeth sharpened to points, voice strange and echoing. "I brought a traveler in so we could finally have a decent meal. I had no clue he would be such a pain in our side."

"Someone should go check on him," growled another, this one a gaunt head with dull, bored eyes. "He's not a real priest, so maybe he grew tired of praying and fell asleep."

One of the female heads — the same that had spoken before — giggled excitedly and zoomed away toward the house. Isogai plastered himself against a tree in the hopes that she wouldn't spot him.

"Anyway," Takahashi continued, "it'll all be worth it in the end. It's been so long since I've had a human. If I must spend some hours stuck waiting outside in exchange for flesh, I am willing."

Isogai moaned, guessing Takahashi eagerly anticipated the taste of human flesh. Isogai had no intention of being eaten.

The female head flew back in a panic, gibbering over her own words.

"Hush!" rumbled the angry head. "What's wrong?"

"The wanderer. He's missing! And Takahashi,

your body is gone, too!"

At that, Takahashi screamed in rage, the cry like several men and women weeping and wailing. It caused Isogai to stumble back, stunned, crashing into the sticks and leaves on the ground. Suddenly, each of the floating heads snapped to look at him, the whites of their eyes eerily visible in the night's darkness, trained on him, silent as the grave.

"There you are!" snarled Takahashi. "Where is my body?"

Each head began to gibber and wail, but Isogai was a man of strong will, and he dared not let his fear paralyze him again. A head flew at him, its mouth opened unnaturally, teeth ready to tear into his neck, but he swiped it from the air with his hanbo, feeling a satisfying crack of the wood against the monster's skull.

Pandemonium broke then and there, as every head darted for Isogai. He had survived worse than this, and he struck again and again at the heads, narrowly avoiding death and crippling pain several times. At some point, he struck one of the heads so hard it flew into a tree. Glancing at his hanbo, he saw several sharp teeth embedded in his weapon.

The heads relented, still screaming, now with confusion and frustration in the midst of their hellish voices. They flitted away, leaving Isogai. All, except for Takahashi.

"Where is it?" the woodcutter continued to scream. "Where is my body?" He flew forward, sharp-as-knives teeth gnashing.

Isogai said nothing, barely able to keep away from this last attacking head. He knew what this creature was — a yōkai called nukekubi. And he also knew that if a nukekubi could not find its body again, it would eventually die.

"I've prayed for your good fortune, but I don't believe that will be enough to lift this curse you wretched thing!" Isogai took one large swing with his hanbo, but missed, Takahashi dancing around it. The evil head flew forward, ready to sink teeth into Isogai's neck.

Isogai stepped out of the way, letting the woodcutter bite into a tree instead. He smashed it across the back of the skull one last time, and Takahashi's head fell to the ground, dead as far as he could tell.

He walked back inside the house, amused once more that night. Inside, the other nukekubi had just finished reattaching themselves to their bodies. They took one look at Isogai and, terrified of the man, ran away, their faces pulpy and bruised from his hanbo.

Isogai's stomach growled, and he sighed, feeling much more at peace with the state of the house. He locked himself back in his guest room and soon fell asleep, quite certain that no other goblins, demons, or ghosts would bother with him that night.

化け草履

Illustration 5: Bakezori

Walk The Mighty

by D.C. McGannon

Yokai: Bakezori

In the famous musical *Les Misérables*, the boy Gavroche sings his well-known song, *Little People*. There is a line that says, *"A flea can bite the bottom of the Pope in Rome!"*

This line sprung to mind when writing this story. It's the tale of a tiny pair of slippers who are discarded but go on to become the mightiest of servants, and in this case, mighty protectors.

Sometimes, yokai *do* teach us very important lessons. Here, that lesson is that even the smallest in our world hold great value, and that we should be mindful to care for all living things in our universe. And also, that we should be content with what we have and seek to help others in need.

Walk The Mighty

by D.C. McGannon

In a time not too unlike our own, a family with meager means became a bitter and unsavory people — thankless in every way. They amassed things they did not need, with resources they did not have. They borrowed and became slaves to their desires, forgetting to appreciate what they had and to be satisfied with the little things in life.

As oft they did, the poor family discarded many things that were still useful, while coveting newer items. Bright things. Things which shined and made a preferred statement over their previous, more practical possessions.

On any given day, they would throw out clothing, or cookware, or simple wooden toys, all of which still had much life to live. In doing so, the spirits of these items would awake and become aware of their dispossessed states, longing to be possessed again.

One particular day, the unappreciative family threw out all their slippers and sandals, though they still had many more steps to take and many more miles to journey. Most of the slippers and sandals became angry upon waking, or disenchanted, or just downright sarcastic. As such, they would play tricks on anyone who crossed their paths, biting people's toes, or crossing their feet, tripping them on their way.

One pair of slippers, however, remained sad, for the slippers found great pleasure in serving their master. Now, without anyone to serve — no one to protect over the rocky ground, or to keep warm on cold nights, or to protect from puddles on rainy days — the disembodied slippers remained melancholy, wishing for the opportunity to possess a master once more.

As it happens, their wish would soon be granted.

A local governor — a kind leader filled with compassion and a desire to find a place and purpose for every person and every thing under his rule — decreed that the servants and staff of his own house would gather and collect discarded items and find ways for them to be used again. He did the very same for people who were discarded by society as well. Some tended gardens, while others prepared meals, while yet others tended to the rice harvest and stores. All were given a task to complete, a safe place to lay their head, and were celebrated as a vibrant part of their community.

Because of this, the governor's lands became wealthy and the people under his leadership were healthy and happy.

As for household items, or clothing, or furniture that had been discarded, they might find new life as art, or refurbished gifts to those in need.

A day not too far off from their discarding, the disconsolate slippers were discovered by a servant of the governor's house, and brought back to be stitched, and for their soles to be strengthened. New cloth covered the slippers, and fresh ribbons were fastened securely to their tops. With their surface cleaned and well-presented, the slippers' spirits were quickened.

Now, as our tale suggests, the governor's feet were diminutive in size and strength, and required well-crafted and properly-sized coverings. It so happens that our newly-spirited slippers were a perfect fit. And so, these once-discarded, sad slippers, who had been thrown out and forgotten by one of the lowliest, and most ungrateful families in the land had been rescued and placed in the refuge of the most prestigious home, and in the personal service of the governor himself.

Some time passed and the slippers were joyful, having been granted their wish to protect a master once more.

Hard times, however, eventually beset and devoured the land, causing great need and hardship among the people. Many sought the assistance of the governor — from food rations to herbs for medicine, and even some for shelter and console.

On a desperate day not too unlike many others in these difficult times, the family who had discarded their slippers and sandals found themselves before the governor, hands out for help in the darkest of their days.

Compassionate and generous as he was, the governor provided for the people in his land. This family found grace in his eyes and received gifts of food and medicine before being sent on their way. As they made their way to the gates for their journey home, the governor noticed their feet were bare, dirty and chaffed.

He called the family back into his court and offered their choice of slippers and sandals for their feet before leaving. They gave their thanks and chose their foot coverings. The youngest of the family was the only one who couldn't find the size she needed for her feet.

Always observant, the governor pulled back his robes and removed his own slippers, offering them to the child. They were a perfect fit. With tears of gratitude and a respectful bow, she placed the slippers on her feet and felt the warmth of their protection. For the first time in her life, she wore something on her feet.

After exiting the gates of the governor's gardens, the family began to mock the governor for having such small and weak feet. They scoffed and mimicked cruel impersonations, irreverent of his condition. The young girl became upset and stamped her feet, unable to communicate with words her displeasure with her family for such ugly behavior.

The spirits of the slippers knew, however, and they also became angry with the family.

Upon returning home, the family settled back in and bedded down for their night's rest.

When all were asleep and content in their dreaming, the slippers who were once discarded and forgotten, yet had been raised again to care for the mightiest ruler in the land, awoke on this dark and cloudless night with fierce distemper and, one by one, strangled the family with their well-fashioned cloth ribbons and strengthened soles. Every person in the family paid the expense of their ungratefulness and insincerity . . . *save the child*.

The child, witness to the most severe of ingratitude and its consequences, gathered her bedroll, placed the slippers on her feet once more, and walked in the direction of the governor's estate.

It is said that, even to this day, that if anyone finds themselves ungrateful or insincere in word or deed, they may well hear the stamping of feet and the retribution of a child's tears in their presence.

This has brought a great many families back to their senses, quickly and abounding with thankfulness.

泥田坊

Illustration 6: Dorotabo

Fields of Hate

by C. Michael McGannon

Yokai: Dorotabo

Yokai are rich in history, a fact that sometimes gets lost in our modern interpretations and pop culture references. While the "biggies" like oni and kitsune are regarded as being well-known and powerful, some creatures, such as the dorotabo, get lost in the muck . . . literally.

But if there is a yokai, generally there is a history, somewhere, no matter how small, behind that yokai. The dorotabo existed in a harsh time when generational desires clashed; elders nearing the end of a hardworking life, and the younger generations seeing the grind and toil of their predecessors, opting to squander their inheritance on an easier life.

Such clashes of strong will and desire are bound to have their consequences.

Fields of Hate

by C. Michael McGannon

The land was not well kept. If anything, the field was dry and infertile, but Hayashi did not mind it for the low price at which it was being sold. This would be his home now. He would take great measures to make the rice paddy thrive.

The owner of the land was a man named Saito. He was an unruly figure, his eyes rimmed red and his hair a mess. The man seemed exhausted and paranoid, piquing Hayashi's interest. Still, the two men hardly exchanged any words.

"Anything I should know about the place?" asked Hayashi.

Saito narrowed his eyes. "It's a rice field. There's nothing else."

Hayashi nodded. He continued attempts at friendly conversation, "So, has it ever had a good harvest? It looks like it has seen better times."

"Bah! There was an old man who broke his back working the field, and it barely provided for his family then. If you want my advice, do something else with the land." Saito looked over his shoulder at the rice field, his eyes wild for a moment.

"I see. If I ever need to contact you —"

"*Don't* contact me."

Soon after, Saito set out, leaving behind a palpable air of bitterness. Hayashi surveyed his new land with a serious look, arms crossed across his chest. It would take some work, but he was willing.

Tired from his journey, Hayashi spent the day setting up the few possessions he'd brought with him in the small house on the land. By the time he'd finished it was night, and Hayashi decided to turn in early for a good night's rest.

Later that night, a mournful yowl woke him. Hayashi rose from his bed and listened. He opened a door and looked out toward the field.

The yowling stopped. The night became quiet again. Still. Empty. A sense of unease wafted through the open door, but Hayashi went back to bed and ignored it as best as he could, muttering curses about wild cats and their disregard for the weary. His dreams were plagued that night by an old man, blind in one eye, yelling at him in rage.

True to his intentions, Hayashi began his work in the field the very next morning, trying to shake off the dreams from the night before. Saito had left the land a mess, but Hayashi could tell that whoever had owned it prior to him had completed an impressive amount of work. He tried to follow in those footsteps, and began by inspecting the field — the length and width of it all. It was a hot, dirty venture to be sure. At one point, Hayashi thought he saw an eyeball watching him from the soil, but he laughed it off.

"What a silly nightmare," he thought to himself, blaming the vision on his restless sleep.

On the second day, it rained. Hayashi could hardly believe his luck at first, watching the dry field fill with water. He whispered his thanks to whatever spirit or kami had brought this good fortune. But when it continued to rain for several days straight, over-flooding the field, Hayashi started to worry. Too much water would make it difficult for the rice to thrive. Every night as it continued to rain, he heard a mournful cry. Hayashi would look out into the field, but no one was there. He continued to dream of the old man, who now began to beat on the house in his dreams.

After a week of hard, tiring, and muddy work, Hayashi decided to rest. He was a man that had known an easier lifestyle until now, and was not opposed to rewarding himself before beginning the next stage of work. The farm was still in bad shape, and he was frustrated with how little his hard work had actually accomplished during the rain. Hayashi dressed and left for Edo, which was a short trip, especially when he found another farmer willing to let him ride on the back of his cart.

Intent on being productive while he was in town, Hayashi spent some time purchasing much needed tools for his farm, including a horse and cart of his own. He had no place prepared for either on his land, which would require even more work to establish a proper place to care and shelter them, but he would make do.

When night rolled around Hayashi took to exploring, observing the many bars and brothels that burgeoned to life. To his surprise, he saw Saito on the streets, but the rough-looking man paid

Hayashi no mind, too invested in the prostitute he was wooing to notice anything else. Hayashi watched as Saito disappeared into the brothel, noticing how the man's eyes looked as red and restless as ever. He shrugged. The man was of no consequence now, and he had his own matters to seek out that night.

Hayashi returned to his farm on horseback, a satchel of tools at his side and a good supply of alcohol to keep him company. To his dismay, he saw that the field had dried more than expected — more than it should have in the space of the couple of days while he was gone. Night had already fallen, so he cared for the horse, and then retired inside.

No sooner had he settled into his evening routine than Hayashi heard a gurgling scream in the field. His horse grew restless, pulling at its bonds. Hayashi rushed outside to comfort the beast, the muffled cries in the field sending a constant chill through his arms and legs. Once the horse had calmed enough, Hayashi crept toward the rice paddy in order to discern who or what was causing a ruckus on his land.

"Who's there!" he cried. "Show yourself. Are you

hurt? Lost?"

The water in the paddy rippled, followed by a long groan. It sounded sad, pained.

Cautiously, Hayashi stepped into the muck of the field. He was afraid, but curious. Though he could see where the sound came from now, it was still indistinct to him. Hayashi wondered if this person was simply lost or some ill-intentioned rogue that had fallen into the field. He stopped some distance away.

"You there, what's your name?"

"Give me . . ." it groaned.

Hayashi, who had not heard the low mumbling clearly, tried to reach out. "Kudashi? Is that what you said your name was?"

Suddenly a pillar of mud began to rise. "GIVE ME . . . BACK . . ."

An arm reached out from the muck. Three long, dripping fingers grasped for Hayashi. "GIVE ME . . . BACK . . . MY LAND!" Clumps fell away from the top of the pillar, revealing a single eye in the middle of a scowling, hateful face of muddied soil.

Hayashi, fearful beyond words, stumbled backward, becoming soaked as he tripped away from the monster.

Not pausing to change from his soiled clothing, Hayashi ran to his horse and untied the beast. He set off for Edo at once, hardly able to tear his eyes from the mud man attempting to pull itself from the ground, wailing in frustration and remorse.

Hayashi arrived in Edo exhausted. He searched the streets that night, finally ending up in the district of Yoshiwara. A feeling in his gut told him that he would find the former land owner, Saito, here in some brothel. He cried out, "Saito! Saito!" at the top of his lungs, trying to ignore the way people looked at him with fear and concern. To the rest of the world, Hayashi looked like a madman, possibly a criminal; his clothing torn and muddy, dirt under his fingernails, eyes heavily lidded after days of horrible sleep, and a look of mania on his face. "Saito, where are you!"

He attracted the wrong kind of attention. A crowd gathered as guards apprehended Hayashi. They tried to calm him, but he continued screaming for Saito, and they eventually drug him away. He was disturbing the nighttime business of the Yoshiwara district.

"Wait!" someone called.

The guards stopped, and Hayashi's head snapped to the figure. There stood Saito, looking his normal disheveled self, a lady of the night on his arm.

"Saito!" Hayashi said with a laugh that bordered on hysteria. "There is a creature in your field. A thing of mud . . . and anger."

Saito's face flushed, and he nodded, tears swelling in his eyes. He waved the guards away. "I know this man. He's had a long journey and a difficult night. Come, Hayashi, let's have a drink and you can tell me about it."

The two men talked well into the night, Hayashi explaining the hard times he'd experienced since purchasing the land. Saito himself regretfully opened up about the nature of the farm.

"I know of the creature you speak. It's a spiteful thing. It won't let you sleep at night unless the rice paddy is taken care of. It won't harm you, but it won't leave you alone, either. I stopped bothering with it, because the land is cheap and I would rather live here in Edo. I didn't think it would bother anyone else, though."

Hayashi frowned. "Why is that?"

"Because, that monster is my father. It appeared after he died, when I stopped tending the land. I thought it was only angry with me."

Suddenly, Hayashi understood Saito's bitterness, the red circling his eyes, and his rough appearance.

"Look," said Saito. "I've done you wrong, leaving unresolved family matters in your hands. I'll come back to help you get the rice paddy in order. After that I'll leave it to you."

Hayashi thought it over for a moment, and then nodded in agreement. He could use the help, even if Saito wasn't good at farming. A second pair of hands would be instrumental.

They left Edo the next day, ready for what lay ahead of them, working the field harder than either of them had done before. Hayashi and Saito both were exhausted by the day's end, falling asleep easily. But that night, the screams of the mud man were even worse than before. It sounded like a man being murdered. Hayashi slowly stepped from his bedroom, finding Saito already awake, his face filled with dread.

"MY . . . LAND . . . ," came the cry from outside.

"Ignore it as best you can," said Saito, returning

to his room.

But Hayashi could not. He went outside, seeing the mud creature flailing about. It was a sad sight, almost as if it wanted Hayashi to come forward. *In fact* . . .

Once more, Hayashi entered the rice paddy, the soil sliding between his toes. He approached carefully, eyes narrowing as the mud man seemed to calm. "My . . . ," the creature groaned, pointing to a spot in the water between them. "My land . . ."

Hayashi nodded. "I know. Your land. We're going to take care of it now."

The creature shook its head slowly. "My . . . under . . . the soil . . ."

"No, we'll make sure the rice paddy thrives, I promise. Saito and I —"

At the mention of Saito, the creature's face bent into a snarl. "My . . . son . . . ," it growled.

"Yes, your son. He's going to help."

"Mur . . ." It pointed again, gesturing harshly at the same spot. "Mur . . . derer."

"I . . . I don't understand."

The thing sluggishly pulled itself forward, thrusting an arm into the water. Its three-clawed hand sunk fast into the muck, rooting around until it pulled out something dirty white. Hayashi's blood ran cold. In its hand was a skull, part of the cap cracked and missing.

"I told you to ignore it!" called Saito from the edge of the rice paddy.

Hayashi turned around slowly, looking between the mud man and the murderous son. The mud man sunk back into the earth with a regretful weeping.

"If you had just ignored it, I wouldn't have to do this." Saito held a thick stick, used for threshing rice.

"You killed him!" Hayashi said.

Saito shrugged. "I left that part out."

An arm shot out of the rice paddy at the edge of the watery field. It grabbed Saito, holding on like a wild animal latching on to its prey. The murderer cried out in terror, dropping his threshing stick, trying to pry the muddy arm away. Another arm shot out, grabbing his legs, pulling him in. Hayashi's pulse quickened as he watched Saito struggle, useless against the vengeful spirit's strength. The son slipped, landing in the water, muck rising around him and sucking him down into the soil.

Hayashi looked away, unwilling to watch the man being pulled to his watery grave. It grew quiet fast, though Hayashi knew that for Saito, it would not be over quickly. He was restless again that night, but not for any nightmare, nor for any cries in the night.

The next morning, Hayashi rose and began to work the rice paddy. He was confident he would reap a good harvest from what had been sown.

口裂け女

Illustration 7: Kuchisake Onna

The Beauty of Vengeance

by C. Michael McGannon

Yokai: Kuchisake Onna

The Kuchisake Onna is well known, and feared. A spiteful, vain spirit whose beauty has been marred, she is not afraid to get her hands dirty.

Haven't you ever wondered, though, where a woman of such beauty and status went wrong?

The Beauty of Vengeance

by C. Michael McGannon

It was strange that the merchant and his wife had been married, and successful, for as long as they had been. The two were vain beyond measure; the merchant being caught up with his social and entrepreneurial successes, the wife bound by her incomparable beauty. One's wealth complimented the other's grace, both of which were eclipsed only by their pride. They kept both social and professional interactions at an arm's length, adding to their image of mystique and sophistication. This served to bring them even more good fortune in time.

The merchant decided it was time for them to relocate beyond the borders of the quaint town where they resided, building a small palace, well within convenient access by horseback to the town and its market. This was favorable for the merchant to continue building his business, yet far enough removed to enjoy the peace and quiet away from prying neighbors' eyes.

"Do you think I'm pretty?" she would ask him some nights by the lamplight of their masterfully-designed garden.

Her husband would answer with a hearty yes, followed by playful laughter. It was the first question she had ever asked him, and had grown to be something of an inside joke between the couple.

It was a lovely exchange between them, but for only a season.

Eventually, the wife grew disenchanted. Before moving beyond the gates of the town, she had been involved in several social activities and surrounded herself regularly with the joys of casual friendship. Here now, in the country, she grew easily bored when her husband left for the daily addiction that was his work. Bored . . . *and lonely.*

From time to time, other merchants and tradesmen would visit while the husband was at home relaxing to inquire about the state of business or some new contract being negotiated. The merchant's wife caught the eye of more than one of these visitors, and as her self-worth diminished against the backdrop of her husband's ever-growing success, more than one caught her eye as well.

It wasn't long before one of the merchants happened to stop by when the husband was not around, and she seized her opportunity to seduce the visitor. They sullied the estate with their infidelity, but the wife, no stranger to the town's gossip, was quite good at keeping her secrets. She invited her prey to return, and her boredom quickly gave way to this new game.

And so it continued. The husband would leave, and the wife and her lover would frolic, until one day the husband returned earlier than usual.

He caught the adulterous couple red-handed. The moonlighting merchant fled in disgrace, never to return again. As for the wife, she levied her insults at her husband in defense of her emotional state, accusing him of being neglectful and choosing his work over her.

In a moment of rage, the influential businessman took his beautiful wife by her hair and fashioned a blade against her face. After a brief struggle, he pinned her down and dragged his knife through her cheeks, tattooing a horrid, bloody gash of a smile across her once-porcelain skin. "Who will think you are pretty now?" he cried in his frenzy. When he saw what he had done, he was regretful, but cast her from sight.

Life went on, the merchant and his wife both broken in their own way. His business dwindled, his own regret and shame eating at him, and the memory of his wife with another man deepening his bitterness with each passing day.

As for the once-handsome and radiating bride, she teased the brink of insanity. She had known unmatched beauty her entire life, the influence of her smile — magnificent. Even after she was able to remove her bandages, she was frightening to look upon, as evidenced by her husband's business callers. They would see her and recoil, their eyes growing wide with shock. Fear, almost. Disgust.

Finally, she could no longer live with the burden. With the gentle fancy of an evening's jasmine breeze, as her husband sat in their garden contemplating, she snuck up behind him, caressing his shoulders lightly. As the merchant relaxed and yielded to her endearment, she pulled his blade from the side of his robe, screaming, *"Do you think I'm pretty?"* plunging the knife forward.

The merchant was able to wrestle the knife away, and tried to restrain her. Like a demon she possessed great strength, however, and resorted to clawing at the man's face in her wrath. The husband snapped and used the knife to end the attack. As the knife sunk deep into her stomach, the wife leaned forward, whispering, angry, "Do you think I'm pretty *now*?"

The house of the merchant was soon rumored to be a place of unbearable sadness. Hate grew where love once kept its throne. As his business dwindled, fewer and fewer traders risked visiting the merchant, as hearsay spread through the nearby town. *Where had the wife gone? Why did the merchant look more like a madman each day? Why was his house and garden falling into such rapid disrepair?*

As time passed, the people of the town left the merchant to his own devices. He became estranged, his hard-earned career in ruin. The merchant gave up, a man at the edge of his rope.

Then, and only then, did the culprit show herself. One night, the merchant lay in his overgrown garden, weeping to the sky. His wife appeared to him, dressed in rich clothing, a sash winding coy around her face. The husband could hardly believe it and ran to her, apologizing, begging her to come back to him.

"Do you think I'm pretty?" she recited softly in his ear.

The husband laughed, a desperate man. "Yes!" he answered.

The woman ripped the sash away from her face, revealing the bloody, crooked grin carved into her cheeks. "Do you think I'm pretty?"

The husband fell back, realizing the truth of his wife's appearance. She was a vengeful ghost. And he was her murderer.

She held a knife, and the husband could only watch, weak and unresponsive, as she raised it high above her head. Two slashes, inhumanly fast, cut deep red lines into the merchant's face. She did not stop there. In the breath of several moments, the merchant was released painfully from his wretched existence, the culmination of vanity and wrath finally taking its toll.

The slit-mouthed woman stood in the courtyard,

lost. Her murderer was dead, but she was not satisfied. Even in death, her image would never again regain its former beauty. She craved that feeling again, but knew it would never come.

Tucking her knife into her sleeve and wrapping her face in the silk sash, the slit-mouthed woman walked toward the lights of the town. It wasn't long before she passed a lonely traveler on the path. She walked up to him and giggled, asking him a simple question . . .

"Do you think I'm pretty?"

百々目鬼

Illustration 8: Dodomeki

A Celebration of Vision

by C. Michael McGannon

Yokai: Dodomeki

Not all yokai are evil.

In fact, for yokai in general, it is a difficult task to pin down who should be deemed evil, who is good, and who wavers on that gray line of being simple mischief-making spirits. It is generally thought that yokai exist to terrify and pester human beings, and that seems a viable argument. However, there are several old stories of kindness, understanding, and, if the occasion calls for such, redemption.

The dodomeki is an interesting yokai. She was once a thief herself, now keeping her eyes — all one hundred of them — on the lookout for other thieves. Some even would even visit temples, learning more about the beliefs and teachings of the monks with a respectful and open mind.

It should never be forgotten, though, that these are powerful creatures. Monsters. Gods . . . *and demons.*

A Celebration of Vision

by C. Michael McGannon

Miya waited for the signal. It was a hot, busy summer night. A celebratory festival was in full swing. Sweat, dust, and the smell of food played against each other in the air, making Miya's stomach growl. Across the street, in the shadows, several feet away from the large lamps, stood Tomo, her teacher, or perhaps better described, her handler.

They already had triple their usual score that night, making in hours what usually took them an entire day. But Miya could see it in his eyes. *Tomo wanted more.*

They had done well so far to blend in with this town of simple poor folk, but after tonight Miya knew they would have to leave. They had picked one too many pockets. She didn't know how they hadn't already been caught.

Must be the sake, she thought, watching one

of the celebrators stumbling by. She shook her head. *Adults and their alcohol.*

Looking back, Tomo was gone. She cursed to herself, having missed the signal. She searched for him among the procession, eyes meeting a beautiful woman in a strange, hooded dress who danced through the throng. She was ethereal, passing through clusters of people without effort, enchanting Miya with every twirl, long sleeves gliding through the air like kites.

"Miya! You little weasel, you missed him."

Miya jumped, flinching at Tomo's harsh voice as he appeared beside her.

"I-I-I couldn't find you. I didn't know where you had gone, I'm sorry,"

"Little idiot. Fine! We'll do it again."

"Please, can this be our last —" Miya quieted herself as Tomo looked over his shoulder, giving her a dangerous glare.

Again, Tomo positioned himself off the street. He gave her another glare before looking over new potential marks passing through the procession. Tomo seemed to take interest in someone. He gave Miya a greedy smile and walked forward.

With a heavy sigh, Miya stepped into the rush of bodies. She picked her way through, dodging a boisterous woman here, a man admiring the lights there. And then she saw Tomo's target.

It was the hooded woman! She sauntered through the crowd, now seeming as if she was headed somewhere. Tomo moved to get in front of her — it was one of their routines. Tomo would run into a person *on accident*, and then Miya would use the distraction to pick the person's pockets. They were good at it too.

But the woman, in her dancing and twirling, completely escaped Tomo's view. He stood there, baffled for a moment, before finding her again. Miya followed, slower now, fascinated. Under her darkened hood, the woman's eye caught Miya's. She knew they were there.

Casual and free, the woman made her way to the edge of the procession, leaving the revelry. She seemed to glide more than walk, retaining her grace even in a simple stride. Tomo followed her out of the crowd, frustration clearly set in his shoulders, though his face was passive.

Miya lost them for a moment, distracted and

struggling to keep after her master. When she was finally free of the celebration she looked, but saw no one. Some distance away, a small alleyway curved into darkness. She approached it, fast to catch up, but pretending to take her time. When she reached the threshold of the alley, a bright flash came from within, along with the brief sound of roaring fire barely audible over the procession behind her. Miya grew nervous, and cold.

She walked through the alley slow, bare toes careful to find each step quiet as she neared the end. When she turned the corner she was surprised to see the woman, alone. The woman raised her arms and pulled her hood back, her sleeves sliding to reveal her arms in the process, and Miya gasped. Hundreds of small eyes covered the woman's arms, neck, and forehead, leaving hardly any room between them to show her pale white skin. And each visible eye trained itself on Miya.

"Don't scream," said the woman. "Don't run. You are free now."

Frozen and fearful, Miya dared not move as the woman walked forward to leave the alley. She paused as an apple fell from her sleeve, which she handed to the girl.

"There are better ways to survive, better ways to live, than as a thief."

And after saying so, the woman vanished.

Miya was left alone in the darkness, clutching the apple with both hands. Only then, when the woman was gone, did she notice the burn marks on the back of the alley wall, and a small mound of ash below them on the ground.

狸

Illustration 9: Tanuki

The Tanuki's Stew

by C. Michael McGannon

Yokai: Tanuki

Who is ready for a tale in the tradition of Aesop's Fables, but with a little cannibalism?

As you should be able to tell by this point, Japanese fairy tales do not shy away from the darker, more bizarre side of their characters. And they shouldn't!

Sometimes, however, it is a little shocking. You could be reminiscing on the cute, fuzzy face of the tanuki, or raccoon dog. The next moment, that same creature might commit a crime so foul it takes another magical creature to levy its vengeance to bring an end the story.

The Tanuki's Stew

by C. Michael McGannon

The old man lay in wait, watching the trap eagerly. He was hungry, and it had been some time since he and his wife had enjoyed any real meat with their dinner. A rustling through the leaves caused his heart to jump with excitement, and he crouched down so as not to frighten off any potential catch. There was a loud SNAP! and the rope flew upward from the forest floor. A rabbit suspended, flailing, from a tree. The farmer gasped and ran to the creature.

"Apologies! So very sorry!" he cried, working at the knot around the rabbit's leg. "Here, Usagi-san, I'll get you down!"

The rabbit, seeing his friend the farmer, stopped struggling, although his small chest shook with the excitement between his heart and lungs. "Oh dear, I thought I was done for."

"Lucky it was I that caught you and not another," the farmer said. He let the rabbit down to the ground gently. "Be safe, Usagi-san!"

The rabbit nodded. Although forgetful sometimes, he was a clever creature when determined. He gave a brief farewell and went foraging away from his friend.

The man, however, reset his trap, his stomach growling even deeper than before. It wasn't long before another animal wandered by. This time, when the trap was triggered, the creature hit its head on the ground and swung unconscious in the air. The farmer jumped with joy when he saw it was a thick raccoon dog, or *tanuki*. They would eat well tonight.

He made it back home in haste, tying the tanuki up in the kitchen by its feet. His wife was equally excited when she walked in. "Tonight," she told him, "we shall have stew!"

About that time, the tanuki woke up, his head throbbing and aching. He saw that he was trapped and began to panic. "Let me go!" cried the tanuki. "Here, if you let me go I will bring you many great riches!"

But the husband refused. He knew that tanuki were mischievous creatures, clever and generally untrustworthy. That, and he was still hungry. He departed to run a quick errand.

"Let me go," the tanuki pleaded to the wife. "I am meaty and probably taste very good, yes, but if you let me go, I will catch for you one hundred fish! Surely that would feed you both for a longer period of time?"

Feeling pity for the creature and agreeing that one hundred fish would provide quite a few meals, she cut the tanuki's ties and let him down. With a terrible snarl, the tanuki jumped upon the woman and strangled her to death.

Hours later, the husband returned. Never had his wife cooked something with such a wonderful aroma. Hungry, his mouth watered as he sat down with a bowl of the stew. His wife watched him and smiled sweetly, urging him to eat. So hungry was he, the farmer didn't even notice she refrained from eating her own bowl of stew. The meat was more delicious than anything he had eaten in months; rich, almost sweet.

Several ravenous spoonfuls in, the old woman

began to laugh, but her voice was deeper than ever, and her teeth were small and sharp. "You didn't even notice, you old fool!"

The farmer shrunk back, growing nervous as his wife changed shape in front of him, becoming smaller, and much furrier — until the tanuki sat in her place!

"Where is my wife, you devilish beast?" cried the farmer.

"In the stew, of course! Who did you think you were eating? Me?"

The truth hit the farmer with such ferocity that he was stunned into silent immobility, and he could only sit there in horror as the tanuki got up and exited the house, laughing the entire way. "You should have never caught me!" the raccoon dog called over his shoulder. The husband starved himself for the next few days, grieving over the loss of his wife, and the horrible trick that had been played upon him.

And that is how the rabbit found him. The small animal had come to visit his friends the farmer and his wife, bringing with him a feast of fruits and vegetables. However, when he saw the red-rimmed, maddened eyes of his friend, the rabbit rushed to ask what had happened. When he heard the farmer's tale, he grew impassioned.

"I'll find this tanuki and avenge her," he told the old man. "Be sure of it!"

The next day, the tanuki was out fishing when he heard the sounds of struggle nearby. Curious, he searched and found a small rabbit carrying a bundle of wood on its back. The tanuki, thinking of what prank he could play upon the rabbit, jumped out of the bushes. "Greetings, friend! Here, let me help you with that. It looks heavy."

The rabbit, panting for breath, made no argument and gave up the load.

"Where to, friend?" asked the tanuki.

The rabbit pointed, still short of breath. "My house. It's right up ahead."

The tanuki nodded and carried the bundle along, following the rabbit. Although it wasn't terribly heavy, he quickly started to sweat. "Has it gotten warmer?" asked the tanuki.

"No, not terribly," the rabbit said, not looking back. "Thank you for the help, by the way."

The tanuki huffed. "My pleasure! But it really

does seem to be getting warmer. Wait, do you hear that? That sounds like . . ."

"A crackling fire?" the rabbit laughed. "Yes, I have a fire burning in front of my cottage, which we're close to by now. I'm cooking stew."

The tanuki couldn't speak at that point. He was feeling lightheaded from a sudden increase in heat. It grew so hot, in fact, that his back and tail felt like they had caught fire. He yelped, for sure enough, the wood he was carrying had indeed caught fire.

"Oh my!" cried the rabbit, finally turning around. The tanuki had shrugged off the bundle, but it was too late. His back was badly burned, the fur missing.

"Quick, to my cabin, I have a poultice that will help," the rabbit told him. Leaving the still-smoldering wood behind, the rabbit led the tanuki quickly to his cabin. A large fire was outside, and a tub of water sat next to it. "Wait here for a moment."

The rabbit hopped inside, returning a few moments later with a jar of some creamy substance. He opened the jar and handed it to the tanuki. "This will help cool your burns," he told the raccoon dog.

The tanuki snatched it from his hand, dumping

the entire jar down his back. But instead of cooling him down, it only burned more, and he howled in pain, "What is this?" He looked at the jar, mortified when he read the label: *Pepper jelly.*

"Oh my!" the rabbit exclaimed once more. "I grabbed the wrong jar, I am so sorry. Quick, jump into the water! It's sure to cool you down."

Thinking only of how his skin burned, the tanuki dove headfirst into the large tub of water in front of the rabbit's house. He breathed heavily, relief spreading its way down his back. The rabbit quickly put a giant lid over the tub and pushed it over the fire, locking it into place.

"Tonight," the rabbit thought to himself, ignoring the angry shouts of the tanuki, *"I think I shall have stew."*

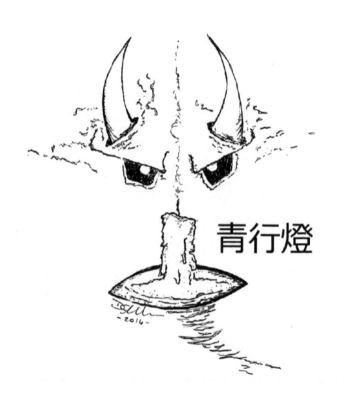

青行燈

Illustration 10: Ao Andon

The Gathering

by D.C. McGannon

Yokai: Ao Andon

Hyakumonogatari Kaidankai is a game that is played using one hundred candles that are lit and set in a circle. Those playing the game tell a story, then snuff the light of a candle at the end of their story. It is believed that when the one hundredth candle is extinguished, the Ao Andon (Blue Lantern Ghost) would appear. A demon so feared, that most of the time the game would end at the ninety-ninth story.

I took a bit of liberty here and reversed the game. Here, our candles are lit by a host of goblins and demons, while they recall the story of a man, until he is face to face with the Ao Andon himself, so summoned to exact judgement for this man's sins . . .

. . . or is it just a game played by *devilish monsters?*

The Gathering

by D.C. McGannon

It happened as I sat long into my evening meditation.

The light of my lamp flickered against the moonlight stretching across my floor, casting an eerily strange hue. Severing the tranquility of an empty mind, I was sure I witnessed the shadows bend, followed by a brief wind of chaos as my lamplight chased its darkness. I felt the skin on my neck tighten, and then give way to the dance of hundreds of tiny hairs across the base of my skull.

"What fiendish wind comes to disrupt my peace tonight?" I thought out loud.

Before the words finished their roll off my tongue, I knew it would have been better to keep my thoughts to myself.

"Damn this night!" I whispered. Again, chastising myself for my inability to contain my words.

"*Indeed,*" a voice tripped through the air in the room.

"Who's there?" I demanded. "Indeed what?"

"*Prophetic utterances,*" came another voice.

And then another, "*This night, damned . . .*"

"I'm mad! What is this I hear? Show yourself devils!"

"*Indeed,*" the voice slithered along the far wall.

I reached for my lamplight and braced to stand, quickly recoiling as the fire of my lamp became enraged and sent me shuffling for safety. I knew I was not alone in my room.

Just as quickly as my lamplight became a furious burst of flames, it was snuffed into darkness, as if by some unseen hand.

Again, the voices came . . .

"*This night, we shall complete your story . . .*"

"What story? What do you speak of?"

"*Your story, good sir. A story of cruelty and forgiveness . . .*"

"*Of selfishness and desire . . .*"

"*The story of your life. And now, the final chapter.*"

"What do you mean? I . . . I don't know what you're talking about."

In that moment a single, blue lantern sparked to life in the center of my room. With it, the strangest set of eyes, belonging to a short, impish figure, glowered in the firelight.

"In a time not too long ago, you were a hurried man. Unconcerned for the goodwill of those around you."

A second blue lamp was lit, barely outlining a tall figure with an unruly mop of hair.

"You were more concerned about your own well-being. Rushing here and there, consuming what you must in order to advance your own success."

A third light glowed . . . then a fourth . . . both with their own demons.

"There was a woman."

A fifth, held by a skeletal hand . . .

"She was in need. In pain."

The lanterns continued to flare one at a time each with a different devil — a different goblin — in rapid succession . . .

"She cried out for your help."

"Helpless. In despair."

The room began to cast a blue complexion, haunting, suffocating . . .

"I remember. I know of this woman. I was

unkind, lacking grace."

"Your memory serves you well."

"Each day for a week, you passed her in the market, unresponsive to her plea."

"But I . . . I —"

"Her body was bruised."

"Her mind twisted."

"Her child taken from her."

"All you had to do was listen, and help."

"I did! I went back after that week and found her."

"But it was too late."

"I gave her bread."

"But her heart was already broken."

"Her child sold to pay her debts."

"I tried."

"But it was too late."

"You could have saved her, and her child."

"My heart was broken, too, after one of the village elders shared her plight with me. I had no idea!"

"Because you didn't listen."

"I was wrong, I know. But I went to her and found her as soon as I knew."

"But it was too late."

"I begged for forgiveness! She forgave me."

"Easy for someone who is broken and dying to forgive. Her soul was rent in two!"

"What else could I have done?"

"Listened."

"Reached out your hand to one so desperately in need."

"Instead, you walked on. Concerned with your own life."

"Greedy. Selfish."

"But she forgave me! I'm a changed man."

"Yes, you are, and that will gain you a measure of mercy in the time to come."

"What do you mean?"

"You may have received forgiveness and pardon from a dying woman — you have settled your conscience in this life — but your next moments have yet to come."

By this time, ninety-nine lights filled the room where I lay cowering. Lit blue though the room was, I could not see the details of the ninety-nine monsters all around. The shroud of fear hung heavy on my shoulders.

"You have angered the Ao Andon. She is here to weigh your sins."

It was only what I feared, given the multitude of blue lanterns. "The Ao Andon? She's . . . she's a story for children. A fright for the storyteller to conjure. She's not real! She can't be."

"The blue demon may be a spook for child's play, but be certain of this: she is real, and your story has caught her attention. Tonight, the one hundredth light, and the one hundredth story, is yours."

Just then, the first blue lamp was snuffed out by an unseen wind. Then the second, and the third . . .

"Wait, what's happening?"

"By the light of the hundredth flame, you shall pay your recompense."

One by one, the fire of the lamps vanished into streams of incense.

"Where are you going? Don't leave me here alone."

"The woman."

"She cried out for you."

"You didn't help her."

"Her child."

"Gone now, enslaved by the cruelty of men."

"The child was all she cared about."

"She lived only to care for the child."

"You ignored her plea."

"I'm sorry!"

"Now you will make your own plea to the blue demon."

"What do I say?"

"Only what you can."

"Help me. Stay with me. Advocate for me."

"We have done what we can."

"The time has come."

The final light of the blue lamps diminished slowly, until it also had vanished. A single prayer that remained, now floated into the heavens.

"No . . . no."

I lowered my face into my hands, weeping.

"Somebody please help me. I'm so sorry. I didn't mean to be so selfish. If only I had known."

I heard the crackle of a wick being lit. Wiping my eyes, I raised my head, filled with sorrow, and there before me, illuminated with the fire of one hundred candles . . . the blue demon gazed deep into my soul.

Awake. Her eyes were alight with blue fire, though whether an angry spirit or simply curious I could not tell. I knew she was hungry for the final part of my story. Was I to tell it, or was she?

Fearful. Trembling. I remained speechless, though my heart cried out for mercy.

I closed my eyes, and the blue light of the Ao Andon gave way to the darkness of the night.

Illustration 11: Kuchisake Onna

Candy-Coated Ghost Stories

A Bonus Story by C. Michael McGannon

Yokai: Kuchisake Onna (Slit-mouthed Woman)

Did you think the Kuchisake Onna's story was over?

Of course not! I told you, she's a popular one.

In fact, so popular, the Slit-mouthed Woman exists both as a folkloric monster *and* a modern day urban legend! She has been popular in modern media, having several movies, appearing in anime, and a boatload of art online by those who like a good creep-out.

Of course, it probably doesn't help that there really was a woman resembling the Kuchisake Onna running around chasing children within our lifetime . . . not to mention other recent sightings . . .

After all, urban legends have some basis in the truth.

Don't they?

Candy-Coated Ghost Stories

by C. Michael McGannon

Haruhi and her friends walked home together from school every day, and had since they were little. The three were nigh inseparable and did everything as a trio, as much as they could anyway. Walking home, taking lunches, studying . . . *you name it*. Slumber parties were had often, and ghost stories were a regular past time thanks to Tamome, the tomboy of the group.

"And then he opened the fridge," whispered Kichiko. "But instead of groceries, he only found empty containers and plates!"

"Dummy!" Tamome laughed at Kichiko. "All of the food disappearing is not that scary!"

"A ghost eating all of your food is very scary!" Kichiko crossed her arms, trying to appear more intimidating than she actually was. It didn't work.

Tamome leaned in, and Haruhi and Kichiko both sat forward a little. "You know what's really scary?

She's back."

"Nice try." Kichiko narrowed her eyes. "I'm not going to fall for your bait and ask —"

"Who's back?" asked Haruhi.

"Haruhi!" cried Kichiko, exasperated. "Don't encourage her!"

Tamome continued, the question had been asked. "The woman with the ghastly smile. The one who died thousands of years ago when her husband murdered her out of jealousy and rage. The Kuchisake Onna!"

Haruhi and Kichiko both sat back, sharing a bemused glance. Of all the urban legends to bring up . . .

"Really? The Kuchisake Onna? The one that goes around asking everyone if she's pretty?"

"And then cutting them up either way they answer," added Haruhi.

"Everyone has heard about her," Kichiko continued. "You might as well tell us about Hanako-san."

Tamome's eyes clouded over. "The difference is *she's real*."

"They're all *real*," Kichiko said with a laugh. "That's what makes them scary."

"I'm serious! Back in the seventies, there was a woman who chased children around, terrorizing them until she was hit by a car. When they looked at her body, her face was split by a slit-mouthed smile. It's real, look it up if you don't believe me!"

"But there was a body," said Haruhi, always the voice of reason. "So she died. So it can't be a ghost."

"The body disappeared," Tamome whispered quietly. She unwrapped a piece of hard candy, popping the caramel into her mouth. "A month ago, there was a girl who went missing. When they found her, her face had a smile carved from ear to ear, and her throat was slit."

Haruhi threw an eraser at her thrill-seeking, storytelling friend. "You're making that part up."

"Am I? She wasn't the only one, either. There was a boy who even saw her."

Kichiko harrumphed smartly. "Let me guess, he lived to tell the tale?"

"He threw candy at her and she was distracted by it. Escaped with his life!" She crumpled her candy wrapper for emphasis.

"Okay, now we know you're just telling tall tales."

"It's true!"

Haruhi listened to her friends bicker and squabble, smiling to herself. After all, it was only one more of Tamome's attempts to scare them. It was just a story. *Right?*

"All right, all right," she said, having to raise her voice over the two arguing friends. "Enough about the Kuchisake Onna. I'm going to tell you a really scary story."

Tamome rolled her eyes. "Oh yeah?"

"Yes. So, the other day Kichiko asked me to help with her homework . . ."

A week later, they broke pattern. Kichiko was on a trip with her family and Tamome was sick. Haruhi found herself walking home from school alone, using the rare occasion to throw her headphone's volume way up. She knew where she was, paying little attention to where her feet were actually going. Closing her eyes to jam out with an impressive air-guitar solo, Haruhi slammed into something solid and unmoving. She stumbled back, embarrassed when she saw the woman she had run into.

"I'm so sorry! I —"

Haruhi stopped talking, seeing the woman had a coat drawn up around her face. She was pale, with long, lush, black hair, and eyes that were intense, focused on Haruhi. Tamome's story of the woman with the slit-mouth crept back into her mind, sending a shiver up the girl's spine. Haruhi heard that question in her mind, trying to shake it off internally — to laugh it out of mind.

But then the woman asked it.

"Do you think I'm pretty?"

Haruhi's blood ran cold. This couldn't be real. This had to be some stupid prank.

But still. If it were real . . .

Haruhi stood no chance. According to the story, if she answered *yes*, she would be horribly cut up, scarred forever. If she answered *no* . . . The woman's hands were behind her back. Haruhi could only imagine the gleaming, razor-sharp scissors held there.

The woman's eyes started to narrow. If she stalled too long, Haruhi's choice would be made for her.

"I . . . I think —"

"Haruhi!"

The woman's eyes snapped to the side, and

Haruhi looked in the same direction. Tamome was there, running toward her, waving her arms.

Haruhi started to warn her friend, looking back to the woman — but the woman was no longer there. Haruhi was alone. She shivered, feeling as if a spirit of death had walked right past her without incident.

"Haruhi, you dummy! Where have you been? I've been waiting at your house for, like, hours now."

"Weren't you . . ." Haruhi looked around, more than a little distracted. "Weren't you sick?"

Tamome shrugged. "Since when has that ever stopped me?" She dug into her pockets, pulling out a few pieces of candy, offering a few to Haruhi, who took them almost too eagerly. "You all right, Haruhi?"

Haruhi nodded. "I'm fine. Just seeing things, I guess."

As they walked home, Haruhi dropped a few pieces of candy in her wake. For a moment, she thought she had heard a question lingering on the slight afternoon breeze.

Do you think I'm pretty?

Acknowledgements

We thank . . .

Matthew Meyer (Yokai.com), for being such an inspiration to us over the past several years, and for the gracious sharing of your art and rich knowledge of yokai and Japanese culture.

Zack Davisson (Hyakumonogatari.com), for being a great friend and an enthusiastic go-getter in the study of yokai and the beauty and mystery of all things Japan.

Matt Alt and the community at Yokai Attack! (Facebook Group), for welcoming and supporting our yokai story podcasts each month, and for creating such a wonderful environment to learn and have so much fun with this topic. It is a treat each time we see Yokai Attack! flow through our newsfeed!

The community at Folklore Thursday (FolkloreThursday.com, #FolkloreThursday, @FolkloreThurs) for your gracious support and kind words. We learn so much and enjoy the interaction with all of you. Here's to many more stories . . .

Michael, Holly, Nathaniel, and Cheyenne through our Yokai Podcast (The Monster Guys Podcast / TheMonsterGuys.com) for helping us bring these stories to life.

Comic Pop Library (ComicPopLibrary.com) - specifically Richard, Logan, April, Lynn, Jonathan, Michelle - fellow podcasters and story lovers, for all of your support and promotion over the past year. You guys and gals rock and we appreciate you!

Matthew D. Smith (MDSmithDesign.com), for your continued diligence in helping our team thrive. Our heart . . . always . . . YOU . . . Wizardly Man!

All of our fans and friends who have joined us during conventions, library visits, and other special events, and listened to our silly excitement over the strange, bizarre, and fascinating world of yokai! It is a joy and a privilege to share with you year after year, and we hope these stories bring even more smiles to your faces. We'll see you again soon!

. . . thank you all so very much for lending your gifts, your expertise, and your community with us as we continue to explore what is near and dear to our hearts: monsters, folklore, storytelling, and in this case . . . yokai!

About The Authors

D.C. McGannon is finicky about his coffee. And loves tea. And lemonade. Sometimes together. He has had a lifelong love of things that lurk in the dark, and is quite comfortable under the light of a full moon. A writer, award-winning director, painter, and doodler, McGannon is co-author of the best-selling *Charlie Sullivan and the Monster Hunters (Wyvern's Peak Publishing)* series for young adults, and *KAOS Obsidere: The Nightmare Has Begun (Dark Waters Press)* collection of dark fiction short stories.

He plays a mean air guitar, and lives and dreams with Holly, Michael, Nathaniel, and their sweet puppy, Jewel, somewhere in the Midwest.

C. Michael McGannon appreciates weird fiction, perhaps a bit more than one should at any given time. It has made him particular, fostering strange phobias, and even stranger dreams. He is fond of dragons, Japanese mythology, and the fine art of delivering timely and inappropriate puns.

McGannon is an artist of diverse talents, and is co-author of the best-selling *Charlie Sullivan and the Monster Hunters (Wyvern's Peak Publishing)* series for young adults, and *KAOS Obsidere: The Nightmare Has Begun* (Dark Waters Press) collection of dark fiction short stories. His exciting new series, *Hollow World (Incendia Books)*, a dark fantasy serial, is now available.

Sushi is his delicacy of choice, if he has any say in the matter.

Milton Keynes UK
Ingram Content Group UK Ltd.
UKHW021310170124
436187UK00026B/1077